panda series

PANDA books are for first readers beginning to make their own way through books.

For Brian and Amy - at last!

Ribbit Ribbit!

ANNE MARIE HERRON
•Pictures by Stephen Hall•

THE O'BRIEN PRESS
DUBLIN

First published 1997 by the O'Brien Press Ltd.,
20 Victoria Road, Rathgar, Dublin 6, Ireland

ISBN: 0-86278-527-8

1 2 3 4 5 6 7 8 9 10
97 98 99 00 01 02 03 04 05 06

British Library Cataloguing-in-publication Data
A catalogue reference for this title is available
from the British Library.

The O'Brien Press receives assistance from
The Arts Council/An Chomhairle Ealaíon

Typesetting, layout, editing: The O'Brien Press Ltd.
Cover separations: Lithoset Ltd., Dublin
Printing: Cox & Wyman Ltd.

Can YOU spot the panda
hidden in the story?

On **Monday**,

Freddy hopped out of bed,
hopped down the stairs and
hopped into the kitchen.

'Hi,' said Freddy, 'I'm a frog.
Ribbit, **ribbit**.'

Freddy's Mum and
Dad laughed.
'Hi, Freddy Frog,' they said.

Ribbit

8

Freddy hopped out the door,
hopped down the garden path
and hopped over the gate.

Boing

When the school bus came along, Freddy hopped on.

'Hi,' said Freddy to the bus driver. 'I'm a frog. **Ribbit**, **ribbit**.'

The bus driver laughed.
'Hi, Freddy Frog,' he said.

Freddy hopped across
the school yard,
hopped into the school and
hopped past the principal's office.

He hopped into his
classroom and hopped
up to his teacher.

'Hi,' said Freddy. 'I'm a frog. **Ribbit, ribbit**.'

The teacher laughed.

'Hi, Freddy Frog,' she said.

At playtime the children **ran** and **jumped** and **skipped** and **twirled** and **squealed**.

But Freddy just hopped.

He hopped over to Polly,
his very best friend.

'Hi,' said Freddy. 'I'm a frog.'
Polly laughed. 'Hi, Freddy Frog,'
she said.

On **Tuesday**,
Freddy hopped out of bed,
hopped down the stairs and
hopped into the kitchen.

'Hi,' said Freddy. 'I'm a frog.
Ribbit, **ribbit**.'

Freddy's Mum and Dad did not laugh.

'You are not a frog,' they said.
'You are a little boy. We don't
want a frog in our house.'

'**Ribbit, ribbit**,'
said Freddy.

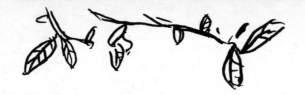

Freddy hopped out the door,
hopped down the garden path
and hopped over the gate.

When the school bus came
along, he hopped on.

'Hi,' said Freddy to the bus driver.
'I'm a frog. **Ribbit, ribbit**.'

The bus driver did not laugh.
'You are not a frog,' he said.
'You are a little boy.
I don't want a frog
in my bus.'

'**Ribbit**, **ribbit**,' said Freddy
and he hopped to his seat.

Freddy hopped across
the school yard,
hopped into the school,

Boing

Boing

Boing

hopped past the principal's office,
hopped into his classroom and
hopped up to his teacher.

'Hi,' said Freddy. 'I'm a frog.
Ribbit, **ribbit**.'

The teacher did not laugh.

'You are not a frog,' she said.

'You are a little boy.

I don't want a frog in my class.'

'**Ribbit, ribbit**,' said Freddy.

At playtime,
Freddy hopped over to Polly,
his very best friend.

'Hi,' said Freddy. 'I'm a frog.'

Polly did not laugh.

'We don't want to play with
you,' she said. 'We want to **run**
and **jump** and **skip** and
twirl and **squeal**.'

'Frogs can only hop,' Polly said. 'We don't want to play with a frog.'
'**Ribbit, ribbit**,' said Freddy.

On **Wednesday**,

Freddy hopped to the shop.
He hopped to the swimming pool
and he hopped to the cinema.

Freddy hopped everywhere.

On **Thursday**,
Freddy said 'Ribbit, ribbit'
in the morning.

He said 'Ribbit, ribbit'
in the afternoon.

He said it in the evening.

'**Night**, **night**,' said Freddy's
Mum and Dad.

'**Ribbit**, **ribbit**,'
said Freddy.

By **Friday**,
everybody was tired of
Freddy the Frog.

They wanted Freddy to be
a boy again.

'We are fed up with Freddy
hopping everywhere,' said
Freddy's Mum and Dad.

'I am fed up with him saying
Ribbit, ribbit,' said the teacher.

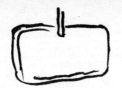

'I am fed up with him hopping on my bus,' said the bus driver.

'We are fed up with him
hopping at playtime,' said Polly
and all the children.

'We must do something,'
they all said.

'I know what to do,' said Polly.
'Leave it to me.'
And she smiled a little smile.

Then she ran off down the road
and into the library.

LIBRARY

Polly looked at all the books.
There were **big** books
and **small** books,
fat books and **thin** books,
books about **gardens**
and books about **ghosts**,
books about **pandas**
and books about **planes**,
books about all sorts of things.

51

'Aha!' said Polly. 'At last! Just the book I need, a book about a **princess** and a **frog**.'

She took the book
and went home.

On **Saturday**,
Freddy hopped out the door,
hopped down the garden path,
hopped over the gate and
hopped up the road
and into the park.

BOING!

BOING!

BOING!

Polly was sitting beside the pond.

She was reading the book.

Freddy hopped over to her.

'Hi,' said Polly. 'I'm a princess.'

Freddy laughed.

'Hi, Princess Polly,' he said.

'I'm a princess,' said Polly,
'and **you** are a **frog**.
We are just like the princess
and the frog in this book.'
Polly smiled her secret smile.
Freddy stared at Polly
with big, wide, froggy eyes.

'I will give you a big **kiss**,'
said Polly, 'and just like
the frog in this book,
you will turn into
a handsome prince!'

Polly gave Freddy a big kiss.

SMACK!

Freddy ran as fast as he could,
out of the park, up the road,
through the garden gate
and into his house.

'Hi,' said Freddy. 'I'm hungry!
What's for dinner?'
Freddy's Mum and Dad waited
... and waited ...
but Freddy did not say
Ribbit, **ribbit**.

In fact, he never ever said
Ribbit, ribbit again.
He left that to **real frogs**.